Abram Lent Smith

Lava Fires

Abram Lent Smith

Lava Fires

ISBN/EAN: 9783337249014

Printed in Europe, USA, Canada, Australia, Japan

Cover: Foto ©Andreas Hilbeck / pixelio.de

More available books at **www.hansebooks.com**

BY

ABRAM LENT SMITH.

AUTHOR OF "A ROMAUNT OF LADY HELEN CLYDE," ETC.

"May we but stand before impartial men."
JOHN BUNYAN.

"Here's a truth that will endure,
'To the pure, all things are pure.'
Listen, reader, to these words; they are Divine!
If my pictures are well done,
Blame me not, O gentle one;
I have merely painted natures, yours and mine!"
AUTHOR.

NEW YORK:

G. W. Dillingham, Publisher,
SUCCESSOR TO G. W. CARLETON & CO.
MDCCCLXXXVIII.

TROW'S
PRINTING AND BOOKBINDING COMPANY,
NEW YORK.

THIS BOOK IS HUMBLY AND RESPECTFULLY

DEDICATED

TO THAT HOARY-HEADED POTENTATE

TIME,

BY HIS PRODIGAL PROTEGÈ

THE AUTHOR.

CONTENTS.

LAVA FIRES.

MY GALATEA!

"My bounty is as boundless as the sea,
My love as deep; the more I give to thee,
The more I have, for both are infinite."

Shakespeare.

1.

Lady, hast thou no love for me?
Does not thy youthful blood,
Rich with the rosy measure of glad thoughts,
Course through its ways with passionate surge,
In answer to my lay?

2.

Or is thy heart,
Like some dried mummy, wrapt
In cerements of white,
Sad with the memories of frankincense and myrrh;
Thy pulses chilled with death in life;
With blood all hueless,
And pallid as the lily of thy brow?

3.

Or, is it that within those breasts,
Those hills rose-tipped, and redolent
Of maidenly reserve,
Within whose vale nestles a spray of jessamine,
And pansies wakened by the dews of morn,
Rages a heat that's held in thrall
As Ætna holds in leash
Cyclopean fires!

4.

By all the gods, I swear,
It must be so.—Or nature lies!
For how could seeming such as thine
Enshrine within its graciousness
Thoughts so ungentle
As shrinèd nuns, within their cloistered cells,

Dissembling to themselves,
An arid victory seek in their possession.

5.

But Nature to herself is true!
And when in her creations
She designs
A brow such as the Serpent of Old Nile
Unveiled to Antony;
Or form, the cincture of whose purple robes
The proud Semiramis unclasped
To loves' mad plea;

6.

Or eyes of sloe,
Like those with which the queen Erigone,
With wanton coquetry, enslaved the hearts of men;
Or neck soft as the ring-dove's throat,
Gurgling with notes of tender melody;
Or tresses black as midnight's wing,
Such as the wild Bacchantes wreathed
In honor of their God;
Or feet such as Diana's sandals kissed;
Or arms like those with which the amorous Venus
Restrained the boy Adonis from the chase!

7.

'Tis then she crowns the work
With heart of fire,
And blood that leaps at love's fond cry,
And life that thrills with passion's scarlet monody,
And mouth whose seal of chastity awaits
The pressure only, of the Prince's kiss.

8.

And thus I know thee!
And I would shake the battlements to their
foundations
Of storied castle, or donjon keep,
With armories of song,
To pass the drawbridge, whose portcullis bars
My bravest onset.

9.

Lady, my love for thee
Is such as shall endure full many a tilt,
'Til I have battered down the gates of gold
And entered in.
For I, a Prince, have come far o'er the main
To break the charm that on thee lies,
And carry thee across the seas!
My galleys lie anear,

Rich-laden with a costly freight,
To do thee service.

10.

Within their holds lie gems of thought,
And golden goblets plasht with life's red wine;
And silver urns enwrought with minstrelsy;
And porphery inscribed with runes;
And kingly seals,

11.

With borderings of rubies, amethyst and sard;
And gleaming emerald caskets,
Filled with many a precious parchment roll;
And robes of state heraldic,
All broidered o'er with turquois, sapphire and
seed-pearls;
And wealth of Ind, digged
From her secret mines.

12.

All these I bring to thee!
And I would feed thy soul
With red pomegranates, ripened where I sang

In lands afar ;
And I would pour libations rich
Of poesy about thy feet,
My Galatea !

O, LOVE'S LILIES!

I.

I quaffed a cup of lethean rest—
Of languorous rest—
As my head sank low on my white love's breast—
My love's white breast;
And my soul was bathed in her odorous hair,
As lissome she lay, and debonnaire,
A thornless rose from a garden fair.
O, love's lilies!

II.

The spent years seemed as a twilight tale—
As a shepherd's tale,
In the low chanson of the nightingale—
Sweet nightingale,
As our lives blent in the perfect rhyme—
The old, old dream of joy sublime,
When love comes back from the old, old time.
O, love's lilies!

III.

And the planets of night in a tangled maze—
    In a luminous maze,
As a dream, white-litten, with shadowy rays—
    With opaline rays,
Illumined with their glory her radiant face,
And her fair sad limbs in their matchless grace,
Where Love had wrought him a dwelling place.
    Oh, love's lilies !

ROSE OF ROSES.

Come and sit beside me, darling,
Ere I go;
Fling the sunshine of thy presence
On my woe—
I must leave thee, rose of roses,
For a while;
Challenge, dear, the clouds about me
With thy smile;
Draw a little closer, darling—
Closer yet;
Pillow here upon my bosom,
Oh! my pet;
Look up in my face, my sweetest,
With those eyes;
Nothing on this earth comes nearer
Paradise!
Nestle closer, O! my precious,
To my heart;
Pledge me with thy burning kisses
Ere we part;
O! thy breast is soft as satin,
White as snow!

O ! my dear, I cannot leave thee,
Will not go.
Ah ! the gods have lent thee beauty
Most divine—
Aphrodite was less lovely,
Maiden mine !
I am drunk with thy caresses,
O ! my dove !
Life was only made for loving !
Let us love !

THE NEW HESPERIDES.

I.

Ever placid are the seas
Where the new Hesperides
Rise like nymphs in all their natal charms confest.
O! the valley of Cashmere
To my soul is not so dear,
Nor the fragrant groves of Araby the blest!

II.

Free their scented fountains play
All the night and all the day,
And their rivers over sands of silver run,
And the fig and orange trees
Waft their perfumes on the breeze
In the land where dwell the children of the Sun.

III.

Ah! the nightingale's soft trill
Every lover's heart doth fill,
When the landscape swoons upon the breast of night,

And the cypress and the palm
Stand like giants, proud and calm,
Waiting for the stars to crown their locks with light.

IV.

When the night to midnight wanes,
And the rout of wassail reigns,
Then, coy beauties, list to love's endearing sighs,
And their dress of filmy lace
In each curve betrays the grace
Of the houris of this earthly paradise.

V.

Happier than a king or khan,
Lounging on a rich divan,
Where the air is fed with musk from many a rose,
There I quaff from massy gold
Draughts of red wine, rare and old,
In this oriental haven of repose.

THE LARK SANG ALL TOO SOON!

I.

The palm trees were fair in the moon,
And the lizards were lapt in sleep,
And the nightingales song waxed clear and strong
Near the ivied donjon keep!

II.

And the castle turrets were high,
And its bannerets hung on the air;
And the knight was mad mith a glad desire,
And the lady was passing fair!

III.

And love led the silent hours
To the croon of the old new tune;
But the nightingales song waned faint ere long,
And the lark sang all too soon!

SHE CAME IN THE SWOON OF A DYING JUNE.

I.

She came in the swoon of a dying June,
 I know that she came in June,
For the gardens were rich with the regal scent
Of the lush red roses well-nigh spent,
And the crickets were crooning a low lament
 In the arbors where roses lie—
 In the arbors where lovers sigh.

II.

She came, with warm airs, from the tropical South,
 I know that she came from the South,
With naked white feet, and arms and neck bare,
And a spray of white jasmine adream in her hair,
And 'round her was clinging a perfume most rare,
 From the valleys where bulbuls sing—
 From the valleys where lovers cling!

III.

She came in the noon of a Summer night—
    I know that she came in the night,
For the wan lips of Luna were kist by the sea,
And the song of the stars was adrift on the lea,
And the love-moths were trolling a faint minstrelsy
    O'er the couches where red moths gleam—
    O'er the couches where lovers dream !

THE LAND OF LOVES.

1.

Strange memories awake,
And glide at will across the sward of thought,
When I recall the days wherein I followed, rapt,
An alien mad star!

2.

For one was a land of suns,
That hung at dazzling noons
In skies sere gray,
And glittered o'er a vast expanse
Of desert waste,
Where, far as vision fell, no friendly shade,
With smiling verdancy,
Nor jocund stream, with laughing leap,
Relieved the aching eye, or listless ear
Of him who dared these trackless plains to cross.

3.

And yet to him,
Whose courage high these lifeless drifts of yellow sand
Endured unto the end,
There came a time, when, at their farthest verge,
Beyond their dunes,
He found a sudden solace of sweet rest,
Such as the Moslem hopes to find
In Paradise!

4.

For here were cooling waters,
That, gushing, ran in never-ceasing rills;
And green recesses,
Where mute gazelles with timid eyes looked up,
And birds of myriad dyes made glad the scene;
And dark-browed maids, with dusky limbs,
Their earthen pitchers filled
Within the shadow of the stately palm.

5.

And one was a land of stars,
Forever clad in draperies of snow,
Where palaces of frosty fretwork reared
Their lofty minarets,

And ancient Night, swart sentinel of Time,
Forever brooded o'er the scene!

6.

And here the reindeer cropped
The scanty herbage of the drear expanse!
And flocks of wild geese, flying high,
Assailed the car of Night with clamor wild;
And, issuing from his sheltered hut,
The fur-clad denizen of this cold clime
Bestirred his sluggish blood
In ardent quest of seal and polar bear.

7.

And, when successful in his search, he brought
Unto his lowly home the trophies of the chase,
He found a welcome warm and goodly cheer,
That gave him happy dreams in sleep
Of bouts in wide Valhalla's halls,
Where Odin sits
Supreme among the gods;
And, mayhap, stirring in his slumber deep,
He heard the hammer of the thunder-god
Striking wild echoes from the mountain sides
In sweep of avalanche,
Or Skaldic sagas in the runic wind

That hoarsely sang amid the branches bare
        Of lonely pines!

8.

And one was a land of moons,
Where hornèd censers swung within the sky,
Mingling a mystic element within
        The horoscopes
Grey-bearded sages drew.
And from the eyes of dwellers in this land
Looked out the old, dead past—
A cycle of gone centuries,
In which the children of the gods
Built pyramids herculean,
That, hoary with old memories, yet withstand
        The confluent waves of time!

9.

Here I beheld the solemn Sphynx
That fronts the yellow Nile,
And, standing in its shadow, saw
The shepherd kings, begirt with leopards' skins,
Again hold council in their tents;
And Thebes, the hundred-gated city, rise
To Amphion's charmèd lute;
And Israel's great leader stand

Within grim Pharaoh's court ;
And Memphian heroes, in war chariots, lash
Their fiery steeds to battle.

10.

And suddenly a thrill of laughter low,
Like the faint music of a far cascade,
Rippled upon mine ear ;
And as it grew in volume rare and sweet,
It seemed the melody of larks at dawn !
And lo ! a bevy of Egyptian maids,
Laughing and sporting as they pass,
The balmy heralds of a gracious queen,
Who to her bath steps down,
Naked as Niobe,
Peerless as when the Nubian slave
Undraped her blandishments
To mighty Cæsar !

11.

And thus my reverie limned
A phantom wraith of pictures,
That faded soon and fell away
As leaves that fall in silent harmonies !

12.

But last I came into a land of loves—
A land whereof I dreamed, where'er I roamed—
A land wherein my fond imaginings
Found fair fruition!
O, lady mine, if summer suns give life to love
Or midnight stars link destinies,
Or crescent moons for lovers fond shine out,
Then does the radiant orb of heaven crown
Thy brow, which feels the fervor of my kiss;
And throbbing stars
Rejoice to hear the mingling of our vows;
And happy moons reel with delight
As our souls meet!

MY LOVE.

I.

Thy face is a moon in a starless gloom,
Ah, Sweet!
Thy breath is the death of the clover's perfume,
Thine eyes sad as violets plucked from a tomb,
Thy form, like the white calla-lilys' in bloom,
Ah, Sweet!

II.

Thy love is a theme for the tenderest lyre,
Ah, Sweet!
Thou art to my heart the ripe bud of desire,
Unmatched by the matchless in Heaven's own choir,
God knows were I ice, I would melt with your fire,
My Sweet!

UNDER THE ROSE.

I.

Hasten my darling,
  There's love in the air;
Hasten, my precious,
  My warm heart to share;
O! where the moon-burnished rivulet flows;—
Come with thy wondrous face,
Come with thy matchless grace,
Come to our trysting place,
  Under the rose!

  Under the rose, darling,
    Under the rose;
  Come to our trysting place,
    Under the rose!

II

Hasten, my darling,
  The hours are fleet;
Hark! now I hear the soft
  Tread of thy feet!

O! how my being with ecstasy glows!
Into my arms love,
There's nought to fear, love,
Life's full of cheer, love,
Under the rose!

SWEET MISTRESS DOROTHY.

I.

Sweet Mistress Dorothy,
Come, come away with me,
Over the sea;
Long have I loved thee well,
More than my soul can tell,
Come to my castle, love—
Queen you shall be!

II.

Dost know my bride of brides,
Where thy fond love abides,
Soft! I will tell;
Where skies are ever blue,
And hearts are ever true,
Far in a realm of bliss,
Under Loves' spell!

III.

Thither, my dark-eyed pet,
Where Romance lingers yet,
Far o'er the foam;

Where silver olives blow,
Where fairest flowers grow,
And the sweet grilli sings,
There is my home !

AT SEA.

I.

Freely our pennant flies;
    Flaunting the gale,
Under weird midnight's skies,
    Spectral and pale!
Hark! how the cordage creaks,
Answering the ghostly shrieks
Of the mad wind that seeks
    Death's pallid trail!

II.

Fearless our gallant bark,
    Breasting the waves,
Glides like a phantom stark
    O'er haunted graves;
Black yawns the dangerous straits,
Like Hell's colossal gates,
Opening to where the Fates
    Leer from their caves.

III.

Cliffs lashed by crested foam,
    Rise either side,
Where even ghoul or gnome
    Fears to abide.
High soars the Albatross,
Skirting the Southern Cross,
Lonely as we who toss
    On desperate tide!

TWILIGHT OF THE GODS.

I.

Apollo, with his fiery steeds,
Has passed adown the golden West;
But still their pathway burns along the hills;
Now reigns the peerless twilight of the Gods—
My spirit thrills!
O'er land and sea the shadows slowly creep,
And in their far-off realm of azure deep
The stars play hide and peep,
Like winking baby-eyes, that blink with sleep.

II.

Fair Dian in her silver car,
Rides up the turquois-color'd sky,
And earthward showers chaste pledges of her bliss;
Endymion sleeps! Upon his ruddy lips
She prints a kiss—
A burning kiss, that wakes his slumber sound!
O! where can lovelier nights than this be found
The wide world round?
Hesperian nights alone are magic-crowned!

REVERIE.

I.

I stood in the land of Petrarch,
When day her banner furled;
And watched the Twilight cross the sky,
With sandals dew-impearled;
And spread her veil of iris tints,
Athwart a tired world.

II.

Then ancient night, swung a golden moon
Like a lamp, in the silver deep;
And waved her wand, and a host of stars
Opened their eyes from sleep;
And the molten silver Arno flowed,
Like a dream by the Olive steep!

III.

The semi-opened, blushing cups,
Of the Oleanders red;

And the odorous white magnolia globes,
  Their balmy perfume spread;
'Til th' spices of Asia were in the air
  And care was a memory dead.

IV.

My soul drank deep at this banquet feast,
  'Mid beauties of rarest worth;
And seemed to scent the balmy fields
  Of the land of its pristine birth;
The earth seemed very far from Heaven,
  But Heaven seemed close to earth!

HARK! MY SOUL.

I.

Hark! my soul, what notes uprising,
Break the pensive drowse of night,
Cloistered harmonies surprising
Waking dreams of dead delight.

II.

In the dear old hours, vanished,
Strains like these my senses fed;
Hours when blighting care was banished,
Days when youth and hope were wed.

III.

Golden hours now past forever,
Days of joy unflecked with strife,
All are gone—nor fairer, ever,
Floated from the harp of life.

IV.

Soft! sweet memory's chimes are ringing,
And their mellow music brings
Harp swept trebles, far off singing,
And the rustling, soft, of wings.

V.

Friendly shadows float around me,
(Loves that Paradise adorn,)—
Lute-like voices that have bound me,
From the spirit-realm are borne.

VI.

Hark! again these strains come trooping,
Phalanx after phalanx deep;
And my spirit, spent and drooping,
Wakes, ah, God! alone to weep.

CLOSE TO THE BREAST OF A LEAF-LADEN TREE.

I.

Close to the breast of a leaf-laden tree
  Sang a bird all atremble with woe;
And he sang out his heart, as blood that runs free
  From the side of a wounded doe:
For his cry was a call to his wandering mate,
  Whose coming he heard not, aweary with wait,
By the lone nest they builded, with young love elate,
            In day-tide and afterglow!

II.

Sweet by my side, in her puritan grace,
  Walked the maid who had gathered my love,
As a new sun foregathers new planets in space
  From the nebulous star-dust above!
Who drew me as sea waves are drawn by the moon,
  By a form as patrician as lilies in June,
By a soul set to harmonies rare as a rune
            That sanctifies perfect love!

III.

Peace, from her eyes 'neath their dark fringèd lids,
  Threw a glance that was seemly and kind,
As I asked for the guerdon that young Cupid bids
  Souls enamored regret not to find!
And I felt, as her kiss sealed forever our troth,
  That the star thro' the ether had leaned to the moth,
And the new wine of love-life had sparkled to froth
  As free as the fetterless wind!

IV.

As a sunbeam darts thro' the lifting rain,
  Down the night-light, rapid and still,
Came the vagrant, whose love-mate, with welcoming strain,
  Filled our hearts with an answering thrill;
And his song, as it welled from the nest in the tree,
  Seemed freighted with promise of joyance to be,
With the largess of wonder that fell on the sea
  When Venus rose naked and chill!

WONDER IF I DARE?

I.

On a silk embroidered couch
  Lies my lady fair,
O, her dainty rose-bud lips
  Thrill me to my finger tips!
Guess there's mischief in the air—
  Wonder if I dare?

II.

Matchless is her fairy form!
  See! she sleeps in bliss.
Tho' her anger I shall share,
  If I kiss her unaware,
Yet I've not the strength to miss
  Such a stolen kiss!

LULL ME TO DREAMS.

I.

Sing me a song, darling,
Witchingly sweet,
While I recline, darling,
Here at thy feet;
Softer thy voice than the murmuring streams.
Oh, touch the lute, love!
My soul is mute, love—
Lull me to dreams!

II.

Ah, yes, thy voice, darling,
Outvies the spheres;
Taught me thou hast, dear,
The value of tears;
Gentle art thou as the moon's silver beams.
Oh, raise the song, love!
Let it be long, love—
Lull me to dreams.

THEN WORSHIP I MY LOVE!

I.

When habited in sable black,
With bodice deftly moulded to her form,
And trailing skirts that flutter in the wind;
And beaver hat, and gloves, and jewelled whip
Complete her *tout ensemble;*
And poised with airy grace upon her steed,
She rides a fair Diana of the chase—
Then I admire my love!

II.

When garmented in satin robe,
With draperies rippling in rich folds behind,
And corsage laced above a chemisette of point;
Her snowy neck and arms revealed—
(A legacy of Madame Pompadour);
Her wrists and ears begemmed with diamonds rare;
And, swaying to the waltz's rhythmic swell,

She shows 'neath petticoats of filmy tulle
A roguish ankle,
Clad fittingly in hose of 'broidered silk—
Then do I love my love !

III.

When robed in bathing suit of amber silk,
That closely hugs her moon-fed lissome form ;
Her golden hair unleashed from Grecian coil,
And rioting in perfumed opulence
Adown her lily neck ;
Her white feet naked to the moon and me,
Her fair arms luring in their loveliness,
And, like a Nereid in the amorous surf
She flashes from her eyes night and the stars—
Then worship I my love !

A MAIDEN FAIR.

I.

A maiden fair, beyond compare,
  Once laughing sadly said :
O ! love, to-day we will be gay,
  For to-morrow may find us dead !

II.

Thro' copse and brake, to silver lake,
  'Neath frowning April skies ;
We wandered, love was in our hearts,
  And sadness in our eyes.

III.

Where flowers grew of every hue,
  (In sooth it was no sin ;)
We kist the tears and clouds away,
  And kist the sunshine in !

LOVE SLAIN.

I.

God knows I loved you dearly,
  I held you half divine :
I gave you once an honest heart,
  You told me yours was mine.
We met, we loved, we parted ;
  Regret comes now, you say—
Alas, my heart is cold and dead,
          I cannot love to-day.

II.

Yes, many moons, my lady,
  Have waned since last we met :
In Italy our vows were pledged,
  Where Romance lingers yet ;
Where olive-trees and myrtle,
  Love's secrets ne'er betray—
My heart died on its classic shores ;
          I cannot love to-day.

III.

No tender wiles, my lady,
  Can thrill a heart that's slain :
No fruit of love your loveliness
  Can bring to me again :
The trust I lavishly bestowed
  Was lightly cast away—
You come too late, my faith is wrecked,
    I cannot love to-day !

SHE SLEEPS THE SLEEP OF DEATH.

"We never shall meet, love,
Except in the skies!"
Hood.

I.

I madly loved a high-born maid—
(She sleeps the sleep of death)
How oft together we have strayed
Through many a sunny sylvan glade,
To seek some wild romantic shade—
(She sleeps the sleep of death).

II.

Her eyes were black as the raven's wing—
(She sleeps the sleep of death);
Her breath was the balm of early Spring;
Her voice was the birds' sweet caroling;
Her songs were such as angels sing—
(She sleeps the sleep of death).

III.

We read the self-same mystic lore—
(She sleeps the sleep of death)
Could ever maiden love me more?
Could ever lover more adore?
Were ever hearts so bound before?
(She sleeps the sleep of death).

IV.

Farewell, thy grave with tears are wet;
(Sleep on, the sleep of death)!
'Til sun, and moon and stars are set,
I'll not forget, I'll not forget—
Farewell, thy grave with tears are wet
(Sleep on the sleep of death).

O! I BUILDED A NEST.

I.

O! I builded a nest
In the golden West
For my love, my love of loves,
And her breast was as white as the white foam's crest,
And her form as the sea-nymph's be.

II.

And I fled to this nest
In the golden West
With my dove, my dove of doves,
O! a kiss from her mouth was like wine from the South,
And her teeth were like pearls from the sea.

III.

O! we blent in this nest
In the golden West,
My heart, and my heart of hearts,
And we swept thro' a maze of halcyon days,
Now linked with eternity.

IV.

Ah! reft is this nest
In the golden West—
All shattered are young loves' darts,
In a cypress gloom lies a desolate tomb,
On the verge of a tideless sea!

A MEMORY.

I.

In a land of lilied waters,
In a land whose dark-eyed daughters
Sing at twilight blithe stornellos to the strum of the guitar,
There I loved and wooed a maiden,
Lissome as a flower of Aiden—
O! her face was like a poem, and her spirit like a star.

II.

Bright and passionate her glances,
As the tropic sunbeam's lances,
Spell-bound was I by her beauty, filled with all a lover's fire.
O! her voice, like zephyrs sighing,
Thrilled me with its soft replying,
For it breathed the long lost sweetness of Apollo's golden lyre.

III.

Now she sleepeth in the valley
Where the drowsy poppies dally,
Swaying in a slumberous cadence to the midnight's mystic moan,—
And my heart is steeped in sorrow,
And my soul knows no to-morrow,
For each day's returning shadow finds me all the more alone.

THE LADDIE AND LASSIE SAE TRUE.

I.

On the banks o' the Doon lived a laddie sae brave,
  And near him a lassie sae true;
Their hearts were as pure as the great stars above;
  Their love it was tender and new!
And aft in the gloaming, these twa went a roaming,
  When dew was on flower and tree;
And whispered their love by the light o' the moon—
  As canty, as canty could be.

II.

But the death angel glanced with an envious smile,
  On the love that these twa bore ilk ither;
And followed them closely ane da' as they clamb
  Arm in arm thro' the woodlands thegither—
And bending his bow on the maiden below,
  He sent forth the arrow o' fate!
The lassie she died in the arms o' her laird,
  The laddie he mourned for his mate.

III.

Now what was the warld to this laddie sae gude,
   Bereft o' his lassie sae dear ;
He never again trod the love beaten paths,
   Wi'out shedding mony a tear—
Each night by her grave this laddie sae brave
   Would watch 'til the dawning o' da'—
Ane morn he was found bending low o'er her tomb,
   But his spirit had wandered awa'.

GLADYS.

I.

Fair Gladys blew me a tender kiss—
  A kiss from lips as red as a rose—
A kiss that followed me far I wis,
  Far over the moorland's drifted snows.

II.

And with it was mingled a farewell vow—
  A vow she pledged 'ere I galloped away—
A vow as sacred as any, I trow,
  As Brahmin e'er made as he turned to pray.

III.

Ah! fair was she as King Arthur's queen—
  A queen Sir Launcelot could not gain—
A queen whose power was such, I ween,
  As Troubador sang in gallant refrain.

IV.

But Gladys lies in her cold, cold grave—
  Her grave prankt over with Asphodel—
Her grave, whose sod with my tears I lave—
  God wot, my Gladys, I loved thee well!

I ONCE KNEW A LOVE.

I.

I once knew a love that was solely
  Too fair—for the earth and its sod;
I once knew a love that was holy
  And pure as an angel of God.

II.

Alas! it was cruelly slighted,
  And cherished not 'til it did fly;
Too tender and pure to be blighted,
  It winged its way back to the sky.

GONE.

I.

I yearn for faces that were sunshine to me ;
  I long for voices that I hear no more—
That sent a sweet, sad rhythmic music thro' me,
  And charmed with love those happy days of yore.

II.

Farewell, ye faces—poems lost forever ;
  Farewell, ye voices, sweet as heavenly strain ;
I miss ye—there are others, but they never
  Can thrill or make as glad my life again.

THOSE HARPS OF GOLD.

I.

When life was young,
And love was new,
And the world was not so cold—
I often sat with a hungry ear,
And heard dream-music soft and clear;
Such, I am sure, as the angels hear,
When they sweep their harps of gold;
Those mystical strings of gold!

II.

Still life is young,
But love is dead!
And my heart, as death, is cold.
No more I catch, with hungry ear,
Those ravishing notes so soft, so clear—
God wot, those notes that the angels hear
When swept are their harps of gold;
Those beautiful harps of gold!

FAREWELL.

I.

Farewell, my life, my spirit's light !
  Farewell, love-happy years—
My soul is swathed in robes of night
  My heart is drowned in tears !

II.

My sky with sorrow's clouds is rife,
  My days are full of gloom ;
In heaven my love may find its life—
  On earth it found its tomb !

III.

Alas, that we should meet to part—
  Alas that love should die ;
Farewell, forever, O, my heart—
  O, God ! Farewell, for aye !

"OUR LITTLE LIFE IS ROUNDED WITH A SLEEP."

I.

With intervals of laughter,
  With intervals of song,
And pains that follow after,
  And woe that lingers long;

II.

With briefest hours for wooing,
  When white arms round us cling;
With grief o'er love's undoing,
  When love hath taken wing;

III.

With intervals of working,
  With intervals of sleep,
And death behind us lurking,
  And loss of love to weep;

IV.

So long the time for sorrow,
So short when joy's the guest,
'Tis well we find to-morrow
An eternity for rest !

COURSE OF LIFE.

PART I.

"A spirit pure as hers
Is always pure, e'en when it errs;
As sunshine broken in a rill,
Though turned astray, is sunshine still."

Lalla Rookh.

1.

I'm out to-day, I warn you, for the money,
The new suburban, in the free for all—
My, Pegasus is groomed, and feeling funny,
But he can get there when I make the call;
And if you back my steed you'll take the honey,
But if you don't you'll let the sweetmeats fall;
I'm going to ride to-day for all I'm worth,
And break the fastest record on the earth.

2.

Now take the rein, my wingèd horse, and chase
With me the follies on the course of life;
We'll have to-day a most exciting race,
The road with interesting scenes is rife;
We'll lead the van, and take no second place,
We'll visit first a beauty, soon a wife;

She is a Venus decked in fine array,
And lives in splendor many miles away!

3.

The house rests like a bird's nest 'mid the hills,
  And flowers prank the roads on either side;
A brook, and many little mountain rills,
  Make glad the landscape as they laughing glide;
Five acres of the ground the owner tills,
  Another five with fruit trees rolls in pride;
And five around the house is rich with flowers,
And statuary, rustic seats and bowers.

4.

And hither dwells the lady sweet and fair;
  She is a dream of loveliness divine;
Like skeins of sunshine falls her golden hair,
  Her form and grace vie with the classic nine;
Her cheeks are red, her face is pure as prayer,
  Her loving eyes like skies of April shine;
In sooth she is the essence of completeness,
And rules her realm as Venus did, with sweetness.

5.

To one of wealth this lady is engaged,
  He goes by the euphonious name of Brown;
And oftentimes this maiden has enraged
  Him sorely, by flirtations 'round the town.

I think he will be glad when she is caged,
  But little cares she for this prudish clown;
She tolerates him simply for his gold—
For hearts, you know, are now days bought and sold!

6.

But there was one beloved by Mabel well
  (That is, she loved as women now are able);
He was a most pretentious lady's swell,
  With hair and moustache both as black as sable;
This handsome, reckless youth afar did dwell,
  But yet to him her love was as a cable;
She drew him with her eyes and fond caresses,
Her little feet and décolleté dresses!

7.

'Twas in the fragrant month of rosy June,
  He came to spend a fortnight with this maid;
The birds, and bees, and flowers were in tune,
  And sportive zephyrs 'round the gardens play'd;
And often, guided only by the moon,
  Fair Mabel, and her gallant lover strayed
Beyond the call of Brown, who watched them both,
And swore (tho' to himself) an awful oath!

8.

One moonlight night when Brown was rather sour,
  Sweet Mabel and her gallant took a stroll,

And wandered to a most secluded bower,
  O'er-canopied with roses, on a knoll;
It was 'twixt nine and ten, that witching hour,
  When lovers kiss away their very soul;
In fine—it was that balmy hour of gladness,
That poets praise in love's delirous madness.

9.

She was as sweet and languishing as ever,
  And full of coy advances and retreats—
He was as usual loveable and clever,
  And *very* close together were their seats;
He kissed her, and she said, "I really never
  Saw so much impudence," and yet she meets,
With her sweet lips again his black moustache,
And this time doesn't deem it very rash!

10.

Now, was this kissing wrong? I do not know,
  Nor will I judgment pass—for I'm a sinner—
Although I never thought her gallant slow,
  And always picked him out for place or winner—
He had a kind of dash which some call "go,"
  A something seldom found in a beginner,
A certain winning magnetizing manner
Which upsets people like a peeled banana.

11.

. . . .

. . . . .

. . . . .

. . . . .

. . . . .

. . . . .

. . . . .

. . . . .

12.

But, hark ! a step is heard upon the walk,
An unpropitious time for such a sound ;
And Mabel quickly whispered, " Here's that gawk,
I know his step. It's Brown patrolling 'round !
Hark ! hear him to himself in anger talk.
Go, leave me, please, if we should here be found
Alone together, I might tears be shedding,
Because next month there might not be a wedding."

13.

"I love him not, but he's a millionaire,
And maybe I can help you when we're wed ;
Be quick, he's coming, hasten anywhere—
(I would I were his wife, and he were dead) ;"
Then down she sat in thought, or silent prayer,
And just as Brown called " Mabel ?" Arthur fled.

"What do you wish?" she answered, "I am here!"
And pouting, struggled hard to drop a tear.

14.

"Why, darling, are you sitting there alone?
  Now do not pout like that, come stroll with me;
You must excuse to-night my hasty tone,
  And henceforth I will strive to better be;
But Mabel, dear, I love you, and I own
  That when that frisky dude with you I see;
Although I know you love him not, I fret—
Perhaps I am a little jealous, pet!"

15.

"I will not leave this spot, nor walk with you,
  Unless you truly vow to frown no more;
Or angry be, no matter what I do;
  You know full well, I love you and adore!
So if I take a stroll with one, or two,
  Say Arthur, or some other friend, or bore;
I do it to be courteous, that is all,
And you must never blame me, love, or call!"

16.

"Well, well, my lovey-dovey, come along,
  I will excuse you, for I know I must;
I'll strive to curb my temper, and be strong
  (You be the broom, and I will be the dust);

And when I see you with a giddy throng,
  Or rambling out with Arthur, I will trust
That your warm heart and thoughts are all with me,
And that you merely go for courtesy."

17.

"That's right, my precious, now I love you, dear,"
  And jumping up they strolled out in the night;
She banished from her mind all future fear,
  And her rich lover's heart with cheer was bright;
He trusted her with faith that was sincere,
  She lured him as a moth is lured by light—
And both were happy, now the tiff was o'er
(Alas, the world is rotten at the core)!

18.

E'en Brown, who was himself a warm defender
  Of every letter in the moral code,
Once in a while got off upon a bender,
  And wandered to a house adown the road;
And it is said, his feelings, warm and tender,
  Had with a maiden there unwisely glowed;
In fact, though virtue was his daily text,
He was as big a d—l as the next!

19.

. . . . .

Just two nights later when the moon was beaming,
  Sweet Mabel in a dress of lace and lawn,

With satin loops, and pale blue ribbons streaming,
  And floating curls like gold of early dawn ;
Walked with her lover, Arthur, sweetly dreaming,
  And luring as fair Venus ocean-born ;
Unto an arbor decked with vines and flowers,
Where love had dallied many golden hours.

20.

Once more they sat and talked of love together,
  Of days long past, and other days to be ;
Then it was of the moon, then of the weather,
  Then of life, death, and deep futurity ;
But these were lightly skimmed, and in the heather,
  A bird called to his mate up in a tree ;
He took the hint pressed closer on the seat,
So near, each heart could hear the other beat.

21.

And now, her golden curls, beneath her head,
  Lie crushed upon his breast, her loving eyes
Gaze sweetly into his, her lips of red
  Feel daintily love's pressure and surprise ;
Again her rose-bud lips to his are wed,
  And both drift into Love's sweet Paradise,
And all the world to them a desert seems
Compared with the elysium of their dreams.

22.

O ! happy, happy night, so full of bliss ;
O, happy, happy earth, and happy stars ;
O ! happy, happy dream, and happy kiss ;
O ! happy sunset, with its golden bars—
O ! Paradise is not more sweet than this !
There's nothing anywhere that frets or mars ;
Love robes the world with many gorgeous dyes,
And paints soft rainbows in true-lovers eyes.

23.

What would this earth be truly without love ?
What would it be without sweet cupid's arts ?
He tunes the happy moon and stars above ;
He regulates the fires in our hearts.
'Tis he that brings us peace, like white-wing'd dove ;
'Tis he that dries our eyes, when trickling starts,
Hot, burning tears adown our cheeks of woe.
Ah ! treat him well, lest he may wandering go !

24.

Avaunt ! you moral icebergs, get you hence !
What do *you* know of heart, or soul, or love ?
Go lock your doors and count your hoarded pence,
The true gold of the heart you know not of ;
Your heart is sharp, and cold, like picket fence
All painted white ; but mine, with fires above

Is lit, and will be warm 'til life is o'er,
For Love, himself, stands watchful at the door.

25.

You ask me if this story I have told,
  Is my idea of love that's sweet and pure;
I tell you that loves' purest, finest gold,
  Was in these gentle, loving hearts, I'm sure.
But as for Brown, I'll own, I do not hold
  His love was such as would for aye endure;
And though he posed a model, never fret,
He knew not even love's pure alphabet!

. . . . .

26.

Of all the people on this mundane sphere,
  I hate a sneak, and carping hypocrite;
And from them both, God wot, I always steer,
  For neither have a modicum of wit;
There are no names to call them too severe;
  Of common-sense they never had a bit.
E'en what I've said sings far too high their praises,
So they can go to ——, I mean to blazes!

27.

'Tis better to be clever, honest, wood,
  In dismal swamp, than piece of pine veneered,
E'en though within a bridal chamber stood,
  Deceiving, hoping thus to be revered:

For God's sake, by the world be understood,
  Have dignity, if you would be endeared ;
In other words, you'd better live and die
Just what you are, than prove a life-long lie !

28.

Excuse this burst of temper, O, my friends,
  Believe me, you would like me, if we met ;
I am not one who shamingly pretends,
  And often have my eyes with tears been wet ;
Ah ! pride I have, but oftentimes it bends,
  And I've known troubles that have made me fret ;
But still I strive to be just what I am,
And for this world I do not care a damn !

29.

It is the next I'm looking for, in sooth
  I've not found many roses here below ;
It seems to me I've had a wasted youth,
  And yet my hair is dark and free from snow.
But two and thirty years are mine in truth,
  And yet my heart is heavy oft with woe.
O ! for one honest friend, one leal and true ;
My dog's the only one I ever knew !

30.

My dog, aye, Nora's with me when I rise—
  She's with me when I go at night to bed ;

Stands, watches, with her dark-brown liquid eyes,-
For e'en the slightest sign from hand or head.
On rug of fur, at night, she sleeping lies,
So still you'd almost think that she was dead;
But if I stir, she gives her tail a shake,
Stands, looks into my face, on guard, awake!

31.

She takes my letters for me to the mail,
And happy seems each order to obey;
And when she's thro', wags thrice her shaggy tail,
Then prances like a kitten, full of play.
She follows me with watchful eye thro' dale
And meadow, or wherever I may stray;
For we enjoy this golden, autumn weather,
And many rambles have we had together!

32.

Acquaintances are plenty, friends are few,
And very rich, indeed, he who has one;
He is as rich as Crœsus who has two;
But such things rarely happen 'neath the sun!
My dog is at my side, and seems to sue
For some attention, and as I have done
With this short story, I cannot refrain!
Come, Nora! go and bring my hat and cane!

PART II.

"O, she doth teach the torches to burn bright!
It seems she hangs upon the cheek of night
Like a rich jewel in an Ethiope's ear—"

Shakespeare.

1.

Ho, slave! bring forth the royal steed again,
His golden housing don, and silver chains;
Look to his wings, groom well his fiery mane;
His silken bridle use and velvet reins—
We ride in pomp to-day across the plain
Unto a realm where wealth and beauty reigns.
The hour is late, I must at once away!
What! ho, there, slave! bring forth the steed, I say.

2.

Aye! here he is, whoa, Pegasus, be still!
Be quick, you swarthy imp, and lead him near;
There, steady now, my fiery one, until
I'm mounted, then athwart the plain we'll steer;
I'll give you rein, and you may have your will,
There's nothing on this earth we need to fear;
We're out again to break the fastest time
That ever has been made in any clime.

3.

One leap, and he is off; now swift we fly.
My conscience how he sweeps along the way!
Whoa! keep thy speed, we'll need it by and by.
Quite soon we'll reach the castle, old and gray
Where dwells a queen, whose beauty none deny.
She is as fair as moonbeams, when at play
Upon a silver cascade decked with flowers,
Where wood-nymphs dally thro' Night's golden hours.

4.

And here's the grove, the land is long and wide,
With silvery lakes and flowers dispread to please;
(My Pegasus is prancing plumed with pride)
The evening's fresh, and spicy is the breeze;
Like flying clouds before the wind we glide,
'Midst beauty spreading out in wildering seas;
But soft, sweet music greets my thirsty ear;
Now for the brilliant fête, the Castle's near.

5

Within the palace all is joy to-night;
Out in the garden golden lamps are lit
Within the trees, and all around is light,
And up and down the masqueraders flit;
On flowery banks are purple cushions bright,
And many lovely ladies on them sit;

And 'round them gallants gather thick as flies,
And everyone has donned some strange disguise.

6.

See yonder beauty with those coal-black eyes
  And floating hair, with costly diamonds crown'd ;
Dressed in a silken robe, blue as the skies,
  And loose, silk amber-trousers neatly wound
In at the ankles, and with sweet surprise
  Upon her bare feet saffron sandals bound ?
She is the queen ! but no one dreams that she,
Is masquerading as her subjects be !

7.

She bade the throng good night an hour ago,
  And all supposed that she was weary worn
And had retired to peaceful sleep ; but no,
  Within her chamber, nimbly as a fawn,
She changed her state apparel, and the glow
  Of deep excitement in her breast was born,
For she had in her mind resolved to lay
Aside her grandeur, and for once be gay !

8.

No one knew whom she was, and she was free
  To stroll, and flirt, and do whate'er she pleased ;
And many a courtier who had bent his knee
  To her before the throne, now gently seized

Her lily hand without that dignity,
  And with their lips, her own lips gently teased—
Indeed she loved so much the sweet attention
Of these young knights, she made but slight dissension.

9.

A handsome knight, who dearly loved the queen,
  Now strolled up to her, though he knew her not,
And said, with smiling eye and gallant mien,
  "The fairest rose in all the garden plot;
This is the first your loveliness, I've seen.
  Let's take a stroll to yon fair flowery spot."
She gently bowed and took his proffered arm,
Which seemed to her filled with magnetic charm.

10.

They strolled and talked, she seemed to reel with bliss,
  The knight she recognized and loved him, too—
And when he sealed her lips with gentle kiss,
  She felt the shock electric through and through—
"How much do queens and stately ladies miss!"
  She said unto herself—"This life is new!"
And when he kissed her rosy-lips again,
Without reserve she kissed him back amain.

11.

He, too, with her sweet innocence was charmed,
  And gently led her to a flowery bed;

And there they sat, like ships at sea becalmed,
  And hugged and kissed like couple newly wed ;
He kissed her 'til she almost grew alarmed,
  But too delirious she to have much dread ;
He kissed her feet, her limbs, her neck of snow,
How many times the flowers only know !

12.

And when at length their dalliance was o'er,
  They strolled again among the happy throng ;
And when they reached at last the castle door,
  She said, " Sir Knight, excuse me, and 'ere long
I'll come again "—yet she returned no more,
  But fled unto her chamber, with a song
Of love, so pure and tender in her breast,
It lulled her to sweet dreams, that night, to rest !

. . . . .

13.

'Twas late next morning when the queen awoke,
  And after her rich toilet had been made,
She placed an amber silk embroidered cloak
  About her shoulders, then knelt down and prayed.
It may be that her conscience did provoke
  This prayer, for sins last evening in the glade ;
But if it did, she prayed but half a minute,
Mayhap because her sin had such bliss in it !

14.

She then arose, walked to another room,
  All garnished with appointments rich and rare;
Where at one end a fountain of perfume
  Threw off its fragrance on the drowsy air;
She washed within it, and a fresher bloom
  Seemed spread o'er hands and face already fair;
Then on a 'broidered couch of velvet pink,
She laid down, like a sunbeam pure, to think!

15.

Then with a dreamy languor, touched a bell,
  Upon a polished table by her side;
The maid in waiting understood it well,
  And soft as shadow to the queen did glide;
"Ah! ever faithful Zadee, prithee tell
  The captain of the guard I would confide
A message to him of importance great,
In reference to some matters of the State."

16.

Away to do her bidding Zadee sped,
  And soon before the queen the captain stood;
She resting still upon her velvet bed,
  A dream of every essence sweet and good;
He bent his knee, then kist her hand and said,
  "O! queen, that mortal must be made of wood

Who thrilled not when your beauty met his eyes
(Eve's fairest child this side of Paradise !)"

17.

"You flatter, knight," the gracious queen replied,
"Last evening at the fête, you loved a maid
In Turkish costume, who sat by your side
And listened to the compliments you paid.
She was a woman full of love and pride,
And loved you, ah, too much so in the glade ;
Unable her warm passions to control,
She kissed and kissed away her heart and soul.

18.

"And what to-day, care you for that poor child ?
(You men are fickle as the summer wind ;)
Now come, Sir Knight, since you her heart beguiled,
I doubt if one stray thought has crossed your mind
About her ; yet, I know, pure, undefiled
She is as any lady you can find ;
She gave to you an honest, trusting heart,
And you but acted out a selfish part.

19.

"Don't look surprised, this maiden well I know,
I have the very suit she wore near by ;
Her heart burns for you with an Ætna's glow,
And many times this morn I've heard her sigh."

"Hold, queen!" the captain said, "nor further go—
  For that fair maid to-day, I'd gladly die,
Although I know her not, nor e'en her name,
She fled the fête as strangely as she came.

20.

"Fair queen, pray grant that she and I may meet,
  That I may prove my love and constancy;
My heart for her shall never cease to beat;
  I love her for her innocence and glee."
"Your wish I'll honor, knight, pray take a seat,
  And if you look with watchful care at me,
Your little Turkish maid will then be seen;
I am to you the maid—and not the queen!"

21.

"O, Heaven! can it be possible, and may
  I love you as I love my very life?
Your slightest wish my pleasure to obey,
  My greatest bliss to crown you as my wife.
O! love, break not my dream, sweet, only say
  That it is true, and life with joy is rife;
I love you not, O, queen! for throne or power,
But for your own dear self—my passion flower!"

22.

He sprang and kist her where she folded lay
  All temptingly, and smoothed her classic head;

She did not faint, nor even say him "nay,"
  But gave her heart and soul to him instead;
He loved her in the good old-fashioned way.
  She loved him, 'til with love she was most dead;
Ay! both drank deeply Loves' unstinted measure,
And seemed translated to the Isle of Pleasure.

PART III.

"Advice is as plentiful as spring flowers,
But not always as odoriferous." . . . . .

"Nothing more true than not to trust your senses
And yet what are your other evidences?"

Byron.

1.

Who never marries does exceeding well;
Who marries once sometimes regrets the splice;
Who marries twice is under fatal spell,
Regrets too late and sells at any price;
Who marries thrice has lost all dread of hell,
Pardonnez-moi, though this be far from nice,
The fact is true; but if you should deny it,
Why go into the world and bravely try it!

2.

How seldom on this circling ball is seen
A true, self-abnegating, loving wife;
"Like angel's visits, few and far between"
They are; God's blessing rest upon them rife!
How do I know? by observation keen.
God gave it me, I've used it all my life;
Here is a thought, dear reader, to remember,
Good wives are scarce as violets in December.

3.

The gentle voice of loving wife or maid,
Is like Apollo's lyre, sweet and low;
The rasping of a grumbling wife or jade
Is like the cawing of a carrion crow—
The preference for the crow must here be made,
As many men and weary husbands know;
Unable to shut up, like dinner knives,
Are all these bilious, scolding maids and wives.

4.

'Tis easier to bend a forest oak
Than to convince a "ranter" she is wrong;
The last word would be her's tho' she should choke;
Her tongue is so unmerciful and long;
Her temper under headway would provoke
An angel schooled in Heaven to peace and song;
Good Lord, deliver me from a virago!
I scorn them as Othello did Iago!

5.

But no man ever lived upon the earth
Who loved a gentle woman more than I;
Far more than wealth I hold a heart of worth;
Far more than di'monds rare, an honest sigh.
God bless them, for to-day there is a dearth!
God spare them, for too soon from us they fly;

Ay, like life's sweetest things their stay is brief,
And that is why this world has so much grief!

6.

"A laugh," said Lamb, "is worth a hundred groans
In any market—" and I hold it true;
I like to laugh, and sing and shake my bones,
For I from babyhood on laughter grew;
If you like babbling tongues and direful moans,
Why have them! I will never quarrel with you.
But as for me I never give them quarter,
I hate them as does Satan holy water!

7.

But I've a little story I would tell
And have digressed, so will at once begin;
But when I moralize sometimes I dwell
Too long, mayhap, so please excuse the sin;
It makes variety, I like it well,
But if you don't it will not make me thin;
For I but little care about your censures
And suit myself in literary ventures.

8.

Two sisters lived not very far away,
Jane's face was as repellant as a crow,
But that of Maud was like the rippling play
Of sunbeams on a bank of virgin snow.

Jane's disposition was remote from gay,
  Her heart had never known a fervent glow ;
Maud's temperament was loving, chaste and sweet,
Born in a heart of more than tropic heat !

9.

Both of the girls were young and lovers had,
  And both a fortune claimed in their own right ;
Jane's lover, like herself, was wisely sad,
  But Maud's intended was a happy wight ;
Ay, Maud and William every day were glad,
  But Jane and George scarce knew of pure delight;
They claimed one should be sad to be religious,
But Maud and William thought this quite prodigious!

10.

Yes, Jane was meek, George was a bashful gawk ;
  'Twas said he was too modest to embrace
A bare idea, and she refused to walk
  O'er a potato field in any place !
And oftentimes her face grew white as chalk
  At stories of the wicked world and base ;
All things "off shade" were by these lovers scouted ;
One would have thought that wings on both had
    sprouted.

11.

But Maud and William, bless them, roamed at will
  Where e'er they wished, and had a happy time ;

And love's intoxicating magic thrill
  Oft touched their heart and gave them dreams sublime,
They drank at pleasure's fountain, had their fill,
  Got married, wandered to a foreign clime;
And live to-day as happy as can be,
Blessed with a baby-girl—in Italy!

12.

But Jane and George had different fortune quite;
  She loaned her money to him in the fall,
A week before the wedding, and one night
  He vanished, like a dream, to Montreal!
She foamed as if from hydrophobic bite,
  And vengeance from high heaven down did call;
He laughed, and thought the escapade quite racy,
And drives out now with Keenan and DeLacey!

. .

13.

But I've not finished yet, my story for you,
  When Jane was o'er her paroxysmal grief;
Some things she did with which I will not bore you,
  It may bring to your patience some relief?
For there were things that might with horror floor you.
  And turn you skeptical with unbelief;
So I will simply say she wrote abroad
And told the story to her sister, Maud.

14.

And soon there came reply, a perfumed letter,
  Inviting Jane to haste across the sea ;
And also there was in it, which was better,
  Five hundred pounds for an emergency ;
And that her troubles might not further fret her,
  The letter said, " When you're in Italy,
I'll settle on you, Jane, ten thousand more."
Now wasn't Maud a sister to adore !

15.

Jane happy grew, and made swift preparation ;
  Her face was wreathed in smiles the day she sailed;
She had forgiven George and his relation ;
  Religion, as *she* understood it, failed !
She's happy now as any in creation,
  And none are by her prudery assailed ;
She has a little boy, and loves him dearly,
Who gets from Montreal a present yearly !

16.

I know I shall be excommunicated
  By Mother Grundy for what's written here ;
Thank God ! I'm not with her and hers related,
  'Twere better for their souls—to drop a tear !
Disown me, O ! ye hypocrites sin-mated,
  Still I love Love and Charity sincere ;

I'll take my chances with you when we meet
In that last day—before the judgment seat!

17.

My story's finished: waiter, haste, I say!
  Bring forth the Piper Heidsic, good and cold;
You goody, goody people kneel and pray,
  For one who has gone widely from the fold;
I could not if I would, be aught but gay,
  E'en though I have a paucity of gold;
Gray sages say that wealth brings many a curse;
Lay on Macduff, I'll try the plethoric purse!

18.

A health to one I honor—now I'll drink,
  He is a gentleman, all will agree
Who know him, for there's not a single kink
  To pick at in his personality;
I never saw him at a lady wink;
  Nor go off on a lark or jambourie;
Ah! see the champagne foam; bang goes the cork;
Here's to Hugh Grant, the Sheriff of New York!

19.

Do you remember, Grant, a year last summer,
  You met me with one of your horses fleet
In Central Park, I, with my gelding hummer,
  Was very glad yourself and horse to meet;

I asked you what you drove, a skate or bummer?
  You said, I think, but cannot now repeat
The words exactly, but you meant to guy me
And started up at once to travel by me!

20.

"When Greek meets Greek, then comes the tug of war,"
  Our horses moved so swift they fairly flew;
For both were fast and mettle to the core,
  And Seventh avenue was soon in view!
I led you by some fifty feet or more;
  'Til suddenly a big policeman drew
His club and swearing said, "He'd make it hot
For me" but I swept by him like a shot!

21.

He quickly blew his whistle, shrill and loud—
  And as we dashed 'round carriages amain,
Out of the Park wrapt in a dusty cloud
  Two mounted "Peelers" sprang for me again;
"The Sheriff scared my horse," I cried aloud,
  And whistled by, for you they'd not detain
I knew a single minute, for you make 'em,
And can as easily at pleasure break 'em!

22.

We both reined in, the "mounts" scowled black at me,
  To you they smiled, and waved their hands, and
      bowed;

I laughed and laughed for great security
  Was mine, for well I knew their souls were cowed;
They could not take me in and let you be!
  And so to travel on we were allowed;
So much for driving fast with one in power;
I thank you, Sheriff, to this very hour.

PART IV.

"There's beggary in the love than can be reckon'd."
Shakespeare.

"I know a bank where the wild thyme blows,
Where oxlips and the nodding violet grows."
Midsummer-Night's Dream.

"The roses of love glad the garden of life."
Byron.

1.

Once more, my wingèd steed, a dash we'll take
Unto a happy flowery ocean vale;
The splashing, diamond-flashing waters break
Against the rock-ribbed coast with human wail;
The birds from morn 'til night, soft music wake,
And tune their pipes to strains that never fail
To charm the wanderer who may hither stray,
To dream a golden hour or two away!

2.

Agleam with beauty on the rocky ledges,
Fair ocean-flowers grow with chaste surprise;
The shepherd's purse the dainty sea-pink pledges,
And woos her with his dewy, dreamy eyes;
Rich ferns and honeysuckles 'gem the hedges,
And nodding foxgloves from the mosses rise;

And many other flowers—fair to see,
Bedeck this vale—with prodigality.

3.

A gentle youth each golden afternoon
Was wont to ramble to this blissful place
And listen dreamily to each sweet rune,
Piped by the happy birds with rhythmic grace;
Upon a bank of thyme near a lagoon,
He'd talk with birds and flowers face to face,
They loved him, and sweet stories he could tell
About them—for he understood them well!

4.

He knew their mystic language—and each day
They whispered secrets to him strange and new;
And many he invited there to stray,
But none a single sentence could construe.
Some thought they something heard but went away,
Nor cared to try again—alas! how few
Have souls attuned so finely that each word
Is known, that falls from flower, stream or bird.

5.

Ah, reader, yours the loss if you have never
Held converse with the birds, and flowers, and streams;
And rocks, and trees, and happy stars that ever
Link destinies beyond this land of dreams;

The time will come when you will regret forever
  This sad neglecting—for sweet nature teems
With healing words of comfort from above—
Writ by God's finger—dipped in wells of love!

6.

O! go to Nature—listen patiently,
  And when your heart is ready to receive,
She will reveal to you each mystery,
  But you must learn to wonder and believe;
Go with a heart of love and purity;
  She'll gently teach you when to smile and grieve;
And many wondrous things, unknown before,
Spelled everywhere in heaven's mystic lore!

7.

One day this youth besought a gentle maiden
  As pure as sunbeam on a throne of prayer;
Or fairest moon-kist lily bell of Aiden,
  A loving child of Nature—heavenly fair—
To go with him; so hand in hand they stray'd in
  This valley with its beauties rich and rare;
And wandered to the lake—all silver-breasted—
And on a bank of wild thyme gently rested.

8.

The flowers rarer seem'd, the birds sang sweeter,
  The youth talked with them both—the maiden heard;

And discoursed with them, too—in dulcet metre,
  And knew of their sweet language every word;
They joined their hands and lips—the hours fleeter
  Went by on rosy wings—and never bird
Sang lovelier to his mate than she to him,
For she had voice as pure as seraphim.

9.

And thus they dallied thro' the golden hours;
  All Nature was to them was an open book;
The birds and flowers were happier in their bowers,
  The sun with gold immersed trees, lake and brook
The spray broke brightly on the rocks in showers,
  The waves receding rife with laughter shook,
Love shot his arrows thro' the perfumed air
And life seem'd pure as white soul'd nun at prayer.

10.

When love is in the heart, then in the eyes
  An iris beam from heaven softly glows;
This sad old earth seems robed in gorgeous dyes,
  And blooms and blossoms sweetly as the rose:
Valhalla, soul created, 'round us lies,
  And joy from many a crystal fountain flows,
Adream with love, life chords to perfect rhyme,
And earth becomes a dwelling-place sublime.

11.

And thus it was with these two—pure of heart,—
  They loved and roamed each afternoon awhile ;
Unto this vale—joined never more to part,—
  And life to them was fair as angels' smile ;
Their humble home was near a busy mart,
  Yet 'til they died their hearts were free from guile ;
Love led their footsteps, peace their pillows laid,
And children, fair as morning, 'round them play'd.

12.

This simple story—dearest reader, mine,—
  Is true, as well as all the others told ;
This last one speaks of love that is divine,
  And dies not when the grassy churchyard mould
Grows o'er its house of clay ; for it will shine
  And blossom sweeter, purer, many-fold,
When in its pristine home—beyond the spheres,
Where sorrows come not—or earth's bitter tears.

KARA ALY.

CANTO I.

"I am no pilot; yet, wert thou as far
As that vast shore wash'd with the farthest sea,
I would venture for such merchandise."

Shakespeare.

1.

Through royal pomp of purple cloud and gold,
The sun had sunk behind the mountains old
Of the Caucasus—famed in years agone
For vasty caves, where lovely maids were borne
And booty of all kind away was stored
By many a robber chief and valiant horde.

2.

The eve was calm, and gentle was the breeze;
The crescent moon climbed slowly o'er the trees
And washed their leaves with silver, and the stream,
That bathed the mountain's feet, flowed like a dream
Into a lucid lake, whose grassy bed
Was by its waters to deep greenness fed.

3.

A maiden of a neighboring Arab band,
Whose father ruled the tribe with iron hand,
Was wont each night, alone, thro' copse and brake
To roam down to the margin of the lake.
An Emir's handsome son she here would meet,
And winged with love, the little Arab feet
Would speed her swiftly to his waiting arms;
The haven of her love and all its charms!

4.

. . . . .

Hark! hear you not the sound of hoofs near by;
Brave Kossa comes, the Emir's son is nigh;
The green tents of his tribe are left behind,
And on his desert mare, swift as the wind,
He rides, nor cares for nought save she he loves,
His star of stars, his gentle dove of doves—
Nor swifter speeds he to the battle's shock
Than now to her. See how from rock to rock
Bounds on his steed, until the lake is gained;
And not 'til then that foam-lashed steed is reined.

5.

With easy grace he leaps upon the ground,
Removes the turban 'round his temples wound;

Stands, shades his eyes, examines every pass,
Then satisfied, throws down upon the grass
His simitar, and waits impatient near
The trysting place, fond Fazry's voice to hear.
She comes, he forward springs with amorous zest
And folds this desert rose-bud to his breast.

6.

The willowy step, the laugh, the dusky chéek,
The raven curl and sparkling eye bespeak
A grace and wondrous beauty; such I ween
As rarely in this world is ever seen.
Great Allah must have kist her, for the trace
Of mystic sweetness glowed in limbs and face!
Close to his heart, beneath the moon's pale beams,
Lost in the wild extravagance of dreams,
Their troth was plighted, and the hour of bliss
Was sealed with many a warm and fervent kiss.

7.

"My darling," Kossa said, with trace of pain,
"They say that Kara Aly's back again!"
"What! back so soon; I thought him far away?"
"And so he was, but he returned to-day;
Our tribes must join and drive him from his hold
Within the mountains, for he's grown so bold

And daring, and become so wide a ranger,
Our homes and flocks are in the greatest danger.
And Fazry, O, my precious one, my sweet,
We must not longer by this water meet,
For he has spies who will be lurking 'round ;
And if they should report such beauty found
In happy tryst with me, 'twould greatly please,
For we, you know, are long sworn enemies.
And he, some night would from his fastness roam
And bear you back a captive to his home,
To lead a life, ah, darling! worse than death;
And I, of course, would spend my latest breath
In your defense; but what could one arm do
Against this man and his bold robber crew ?
So we must take precaution while we may,
And trust to Allah for a reckoning day !"

8.

Then leaning placed his turban on his head,
And raised his blade up from its grassy bed
Where he had placed it, then said, " O, my fate,
We must away the hour is waxing late !"
Once more he pressed her to his beating heart,
And showered her with kisses, loath to part.
A gentler dalliance Allah ne'er had given,
Their lives were half on earth and half in heaven.

9.

They linger still, O, bitter, bitter fate !
Why do they tarry 'til it is too late ?
See from yon hill, an old man trudges down
Leaning upon a cane, a long dark gown
Falls from his shoulders to his knees below,
And on his locks, as white as mountain snow,
A turban rests, and as he draws more near
His face grows darker, but his eye more clear.
On still he comes, and as he closer draws,
And sees the youth and maid, he stops to pause,
As if surprised that he should see them there.
Then presses on, and when he reaches where
Brave Kossa and his Fazry were, he said :
" May Allah's blessing rest upon thy head
Proud chief—and also on thy mate !
Your pardon for my presence! I await,
Here by the lake, my son, young Saraband,
Who is a warrior in Ben Ali's band.
Mayhap you know him, or have heard his name ?
He is a leader of some little fame !"

10.

" I know him not," said Kossa, " but have heard
Of his exploits, his name's a rallying word ;

He is as brave a chief as e'er did wage
A bloody war, and your declining age
Must be most happy made by such a one;
My heart is with you, father, and your son!"

11.

"I thank you noble youth, you please me well,
And if you deem me not too bold, pray tell
Your name, for surely you must be
A chief yourself of some celebrity!
One who would be the last the field to fly;
I read it in your dress, your face, your eye."
"Good father, hear, I trust for honor's sake,
If nothing more, I'd be the last to break
The ranks and flee, to seek a safe retreat!
No, never, father—while this heart shall beat—
I am a chief, but naught about my fame
Have I to say—and Kossa is my name."

12.

"What! daring Kossa, th' proud Emir's son?
Thy fame is bright, and many a field you've won
The name of Kossa's famous far and near,
Mine is the honor, chief, to meet you here!
But tell me, prithee, 'ere I further go,
Is Kara Aly back—our mortal foe?

I heard to-night he had been seen again
With many of his followers on the plain !"

13.

"Aye, he is back ! but brief his stay, I trust;
I hope 'ere long to make him bite the dust!"
"What ! will you give him war ?" "Aye, that I will!
And when I've done methinks he'll have his fill
Of war, and gladly sue for peace.
'Tis time, high time, his ravages should cease."

14.

"And yet I'm told he is not bad at heart,
And has been known to act the clever part
Full many times, and only strikes at those
Whom he considers strong and deadly foes ;
He is to some a contradiction sure,
Subdues the arrogant, protects the poor ;
A tiger fierce to-day, to-morrow mild,
And gentle, so they say, as little child !"

15.

"I care not what they say, my hate is dire ;
I would to-night I saw his funeral pyre
With him upon it. I would humbly claim
The privilege to start the lurid flame.

I wish, alone, this renegade would grace
My pathway, then we'd settle, face to face,
Our little feud of over twelve months growth;
Then one of us might live, but never both."

16.

"Talk lower, chief, some spy may linger near,
And Kara Aly, should he ever hear
Your wish alone to meet him, would agree;
For he was never known a foe to flee!"
"I care not who may hear, each word is true;
I would that he was nigh, to hear them, too!"

17.

"Thy wish is granted, Kossa, free from bands,
Before thee Kara Aly single stands!"
And quick as lightning from his shoulders threw
The long dark gown that hid his form from view;
Then swiftly flashed his blade, and said with pride,
"Now, Kossa, on thy guard, I will not chide
Thee for thy length of tongue; but haste, I pray,
And lead that lovely maid some lengths away."

18.

Brave was the Emir's son—but such surprise
Made him most doubt the scene before his eyes.

He backward sprang and upward flashed his blade,
Then toward a thicket led the fainting maid,
Who, half revived, began to sob and cry,
"O ! Kossa, from this dreaded chieftian fly !"
No time had he to counsel words of cheer,
But laid her gently on the grassy mere ;
Then sprang back at his foe, who like a rock
Stood on his guard, and ready for the shock !
But in his leap, ah, sad the fate to tell,
He slipped and lost his guard and slightly fell ;
And quick and fierce as tiger for the fray
The fiery mountain chief sprang on his prey,
And closing, wounded deeply in the side
The Emir's son—alas, the rent is wide,
And freely bleeds,—ah, Kossa, far too strong
Thy foe for thee alone to right thy wrong

19.

Now Kara Aly swift advantage found,
And forced the struggling Kossa to the ground ;
Then swift as wild-cat, springing up, he press'd
His heavy foot upon the heaving breast,
And flashing toward his throat the bloody blade,
Cried, "Kossa, I have ne'er before delayed
To take a life, but if you ask of me
For mercy, I will freely give it thee;

Although I know, were I now in your place,
You'd ne'er extend to me an equal grace!
Now sue for mercy, or I truly swear
To end your proud existence lying there!"

20.

No answer came, too deep the savage wound;
The form beneath the chieftian's foot had swooned.
But see, before them both, in earnest prayer,
Fair Fazry weeping cries: "Brave chieftian spare,
O! for my sake, I pray you, mercy give;
Spare, spare him, Kara Aly, let him live!"
"And what is he to thee, my lovely child?"
And Fazry courage gained from words so mild.
"O, spare him, chief," she said, mid sobs of grief,
"He is my love, my life, O! spare him, chief!"

21.

"Your prayer alone, sweet maid, his life shall save,
But he must go a prisoner to my cave,
And you shall come, that you may also know
That even robber chiefs can kindness show;
His wound is deep, he'll need the best of care,
Weep not you both shall of my bounty share!"
Then with his mouth, he gave a signal shrill,
And almost instantly adown the hill,

Dashed twenty horsemen to their chieftain's side,
And one led Kara Aly's desert pride,
His fiery, pure Arabian battle steed—
The swiftest to be found on mount or mead.

22.

"Your orders, chief," said one. "Securely bind
That fellow, then as swiftly as the wind,
Ride after me; we to the fort repair."
Then vaulting on his steed with haughty air
Said to another, "Yonder beauty see?
Go, bring her, place her on this horse with me!"
When Kara Aly spoke he was obeyed!
And quickly all in readiness was made.
His foe was bound and horsed; but his own arms
Alone enveloped Fazry's fainting charms.

23.

He gives the word, then to his charger plies
The steel, and with a bound away he flies!
The band speed after like a pack of hounds,
And fainter, fainter grow the echoing sounds
Of voice and hoof, until along the plain
A heavy hush of stillness broods again!

CANTO II.

"Did my heart love till now? forswear it, sight!
For I ne'er saw true beauty till this night."

1.

'Tis midnight—echo unmolested sleeps;
The moonlight down the mountain gorges creeps;
And on the silvery stream, in beauty glows,
That near the robbers fastness gently flows.

2.

The outmost guards before the cavern pace,
And scan with eagle-eye each shadowy place;
While 'round about the entrance to the cave,
That seems as dark and gloomy as the grave,
A double guard is set, and pacing slow,
Like faithful bloodhounds back and forward go.

3.

Within the fortress all are fast asleep,
Save Kara Aly; who, in study deep,

Sits all alone, within his spacious room,
As cold and sternly silent as the tomb !
Bright silver lamps hang from the ceiling low,
And o'er the robber chieftain weirdly throw
A mellow light, revealing trophies rare
Adorning the apartment, everywhere.
Rich leopard skins lay thickly all around,
And cover every space of stony ground ;
While costly silks hang from the rocky walls,
And cloths, gold-hangings, fans and costly shawls,
Are strewn around with taste at either hand,
By this proud, handsome chief of robber band.

4.

His couch of silk and leopard skins was made,
And on it, like a rose-bud, Fazry laid.
Sweet sleep had poured his poppies 'round the bed,
And o'er her tear-wet eyes his dews had spread.
She, all forgetful, there a captive lay.
Her soul adream, was wandering far away
In happy tryst, clasped in her lover's arms,
Safe from all sorrow and the world's alarms ;
And felt in dreams his soft and tender kiss,
And garlands plucked of visionary bliss.

5.

Long sat the chief and watched her silently.
Then rose, walked to the couch to better see

His precious prize ; then drew the skins apace,
That he might see her marvelous wealth of grace.
Entranced he stood—in innocence she lay,
The fairest, finest dream of moulded clay
His eyes had ever rested on before ;
She seemed an angel from the heav'nly shore ;
A fair creation ; born of grace and love ;
A rose dropped from elysian fields above.

6.

He stood enamored ; pure as morning she
Lay in her sweetness, all unconsciously,
And slept as peacefully as angel guest,
Or little babe rocked on its mother's breast ;
She slumbered, knit in dreams of perfect bliss,
Nor waked at Kara Aly's fervent kiss !
He gently drew the coverings o'er the child,
Nor laid rude hands on one so pure and mild ;
Returned to a divan in reverie deep,
And pondering long, at last, feel fast asleep ;
Nor waked until the sun, with floods of gold,
Fell lavishly on mountain, plain and wold.
And when he did, it was from troubled dream ;
Up springing to his feet, with eyes agleam,
He wildly stared as if some foe were near
To rob him of the prize he held so dear.

7.

The noise from Fazry's eyes brushed sleep away,
And pale and trembling, like a frightened fay,
She held both hands as if in prayer for aid ;
But Kara Aly said : "Be not afraid,
My lovely child, no harm shall come to you ;
The chief has said it, you can count it true."

8.

"Then why, O chief, am I a captive here ?
And where is Kossa ? If as you appear
So kind and gentle let us haste away,
And for your soul each morn a prayer I'll say."

9.

"Pale Moon you are no captive—your sweet will,
Is my command ; you 'bide a guest, until
You shall depart to leave me here alone
(Ah, mind me not, bright dreams before have flown).
Speak out thy heart, my child, be not afraid ;
No wish of yours shall here be disobeyed."

10.

"Kind chief, I thank you, and your words so thrill
And my poor heart to overflowing fill

With gratitude so deep I cannot find
Words fit to thank you in my troubled mind.
But, prithee, leave me for a little while,
And if you would find favor in my smile,
Return yourself, have Kossa brought here too;
There maybe something for him I can do."

11.

The chieftain sighed: "Ah, maiden, love like thine
Were worth a kingdom could I call it mine!
Your wish is granted; have no troubled thought,
Thy lover, Kossa, shall be hither brought."
So saying, quickly passed out from the room,
And left her all alone—with heart of gloom.

12.

Then Fazry from the downy couch arose,
And all excitement donned, with haste, her clothes;
Then sat down dreamily, with anxious fear,
Her lover's face to see, his voice to hear.
Nor had she long to wait! the hangings wide
Soon by two girls were quickly drawn aside,
And Kara Aly entered, bowing low
To Fazry, with a brow presaging woe!

Two men bore Kossa on a couch, and laid
Him gently down beside the waiting maid ;
Then one swift look upon their chief they cast,
And left—the curtains closing as they pass'd.

13.

Pale Fazry sprang beside her lover true ;
Then gave one piercing shriek, and backward drew
In horror ; for upon the soft fur bed
The Emirs' only son lay cold and dead !

14.

The robber chief sprang close to Fazry's side,
And gently said : " Forgive ! O deserts' pride ;
I knew not of his death—for I would fain
Have brought him living to your side again.
The best of care he had, that he might live ;
For I intended freely to forgive
The bitter hatred that he bore to me. ..
And glad was I, my child, that liberty
Was in my power to proffer ; but you see
Great Allah wills it otherwise to be !
Believe me, Fazry, if I could awake
That noble soul to life, his place I'd take,
And gladly do it, for your precious sake ;
For life has not been strewn with roses, sweet,
And often on the battle field I greet

Death with a cheerful smile in thickest fight.
I would be glad if I were dead to-night!"

15.

The stricken maid gazed at him mournfully,
And said, with eyes awet, "O let me be
Alone awhile with my dead love I pray.
The chieftain bowed and sadly walked away;
Nor trespassed further on her poignant grief
'Til after her pent heart had found relief
In bitter tears, and calm her mind had grown.
Then with a heart of love and faltering tone
Went to her; said, "forgive me, if you can!
Our fight, sweet maid, was equal—man to man,
Advantageless I stood—he was my foe;
And yet I'm sorry that I dealt the blow!"

16.

"He was impetuous chief; nor do I blame!
No fairness, unextended, could he claim.
I know he would have killed you if he could;
His hatred well I knew you understood;
And much I've marveled that you could be good.
They taught me you were savage, heartless, cold,
A fierce, blood-thirsty, daring robber bold.

Though Kossa's dead, and my lone heart has grieved,
Believe me, chief, I'm glad to be deceived.
You are not fierce and bold ; but like my love,
As brave as lion, gentle as the dove !
My soul seems sadly light, my eye is clear,
I hate you not, O chief ! but much revere.
But why waste all your years 'mid scenes of strife ?
I would that prayer of mine could change your life !"

17.

"O moon of moons ! could seraph intercede
In my behalf with you, this life I lead
I'd fling aside to-morrow, and would sail
Across the seas, where summers never fail,
And build a home in some Hesperian vale ;
Where, heart to heart united, we could dwell
In dreams too tender, love, for tongue to tell.
And when the love-wing'd years had rolled away
And we, together, darling, should grow gray,
And Azrael—that messenger of death,
Should bring to us at last immortal breath,
Together still we'd roam 'neath happier skies
That hover like soft dreams o'er Paradise.
O, my sleek antelope ! my sweet gazelle !
I love you more than earthly tongue can tell.

Love me a little, dearest, and I swear
By sun, and moon and stars, that you shall share
With me, a life from pain and sorrow free ;
A life, my heart, of pure felicity !
But Fazry, should it be my bitter fate,
That I must only share your kindly hate,
And you at once would to your tents away ;
Speak love! I am resigned and will obey !"

18.

Each word fell deeply in the maiden's heart,
And sad, mysterious tears, began to start
From her fair eyes, and course adown each cheek,
Before the chief's warm heart had ceased to speak.
She ne'er before had heard such words addressed
To her. Not e'en from Kossa fiery breast ;
Although his love was tender, warm and true,
Yet Kara Aly's love seemed strangely new.
It was so warm and wild, delirous, sweet !
What could she do, but raise her lips to meet
The fiery pressure of the chieftain's kiss,
And Allah joined their hearts, and gave them bliss.

19.

Dear reader, little more is there to say :
With untold wealth this mountain chief one day

Sailed with sweet Fazry to a country fair,
And builded her a home beyond compare;
Close by a river, in a sylvan dell,
Where they in peace and happiness did dwell.

20.

Nor had she ever cause her step to rue,
He proved to her a husband tender, true,
And faithful, loving, to the very last!
And when to happier clime his soul had past,
She wept as if her heart in twain would break.
'Til one night, as she lay in tears, awake,
An angel came, and said: "Allay thy fears;
Thy love is happy, far beyond the spheres!
(The living weep, the dead are free from tears)"
The angel healed her heart and wiped her eyes,
And led her to the fields of Paradise.

THE END.

www.ingramcontent.com/pod-product-compliance
Lightning Source LLC
Chambersburg PA
CBHW032018010726
47493CB00007B/2455
* 9 7 8 3 3 3 7 2 4 9 0 1 4 *